HERE COMES
NODDY
AGAIN!

by Enid Blyton

First published in the UK by HarperCollins Children's Books in 2011
1 3 5 7 9 10 8 6 4 2
ISBN: 978-0-00-736650-7
A CIP catalogue record for this title is available from the British Library.

Printed and bound in China

HERE COMES NODDY AGAIN!

by Enid Blyton

Contents

THREE UGLY FACES SUDDENLY APPEARED IN THE LIGHT
OF THE CAR'S LAMPS

—⁓ 1 ⁓—

NODDY IS ALWAYS BUSY

EVERYONE in Toyland knew little Noddy and his red and yellow car. They always used to wave to him when he drove down the streets with a passenger in his little taxi.

"There goes the little nodding man! Who's he taking to the station this morning?"

"It's Mr Tubby, the teddy bear. My goodness, if that bear gets any fatter he won't be able to get out of the car!"

"Parp-parp!" went Noddy's horn as he hooted at three little dolls in the road. They scuttled out of the way quickly.

"Goodness! There goes Noddy and his taxi! Look at his head nid-nodding as he drives. And did you hear the little bell jingling on his hat?"

Up and down Toyland went little Noddy in his car, taking people here, there and everywhere.

He took Mary Mouse to catch the train one day – and dear me, when she wanted to take her six mouse children, too, little Noddy didn't know *what* to do.

So in the end he made the mice sit on the back of the car – just look at them! They squeaked with excitement all the way. One of them was so excited that he slid right off and landed in an

enormous puddle. Noddy had
to turn the car round and go
all the way back to get him dried.

Once, Noddy took the skittles out to the
country for a picnic. It was a very, very tight
squeeze to get them all in the car beside him.

Another time he took a toy dog, who saw a
toy cat in the street and jumped right out of the
car to chase her. By the time Noddy had stopped
the car and looked round they were nowhere to
be seen. So he lost that passenger and didn't get
any money.

"I shan't take dogs again," said Noddy to himself. "Hello, who's this wanting a taxi?"

It was one of the elephants out of Noah's Ark. He had got the day off for a holiday and he wanted to go into the wood and try to knock down trees.

"That's what real elephants do," he told Noddy, trying to get into the car. "I'm going to knock down trees, too, just to show everyone I'm as good as a real elephant."

Noddy was alarmed. "You don't need to knock down trees for that," he said. "That's silly and dangerous. I won't have you knocking down trees."

The elephant tried to climb into the car, but Noddy pushed him out. "I'll get hold of your car with my trunk and stop you driving!" said the bad elephant. "Let me in. I might even lift up your car in my trunk and drop it down *hard.*"

"You're a very bad elephant," said Noddy fiercely. "I shall tell Mr Noah!"

The elephant pushed little Noddy hard till he was all squashed up in

THE DOOR OF THE CAR BURST OPEN

his driving seat. Then he sat down so suddenly that the door of the car burst open. It wouldn't shut.

"Please get out," begged little Noddy. "You will break my car. I'm not going to let you knock down trees."

But the elephant wouldn't get out, and he made Noddy start the car. Noddy's head nodded sadly as he drove slowly down the street. Whatever was he to do?

"This is wonderful," said the elephant, enjoying himself. "I've never been in a car before. Oh, how nice it is — bumpity-bumpity-bumpity-bump! Can I sound the hooter?"

"No, you can't," said Noddy. But the elephant did, of course, and everybody jumped dreadfully as Noddy's car went along hooting loudly all the time.

Then the elephant got tired of that and settled down to have a nap. Noddy looked at him. Ah! His eyes were closed. A little snore came out of his mouth. Noddy smiled to himself. He knew what to do!

Carefully he turned the car around and went back into Toyland. He drove right up to the big Noah's Ark. Mr Noah was there, and Noddy beckoned to him.

"This elephant has been very bad," said little Noddy. "He tried to make me take him to the woods to knock down trees. Please will you tell him off, Mr Noah?"

"Certainly, certainly, certainly!" said Mr Noah, and he tapped the big elephant smartly on the trunk. The toy animal opened his eyes with a jump.

"Out you get, elephant," said Mr Noah sternly. "What's this I hear about you? Go into the ark, put yourself in a corner – and WAIT FOR ME TO COME!"

Oh dear, oh dear! You should have seen that elephant. He got out of the car, hung his head down and lumbered into the ark. He knew what to expect from Mr Noah!

"Thanks, Mr Noah," said Noddy, turning the car around again. "Let me know when you and Mrs Noah want a ride. I'll take you in my car!"

And off he went, very pleased to have got rid of the big, bad elephant!

—⁕ 2 ⁕—

NODDY AND THE CLOCKWORK CLOWN

NODDY was always pleased when his day's work was done and he could drive home to his little house. He had a dear little home, which he and his friend Big-Ears had made together, out of toy bricks. Isn't it nice? It's called House-for-One because it is so small.

It didn't have a garage at first. When Noddy had saved a little money he went and got some more toy bricks in a box.

Then he took them out and built the tiny garage at the side of House-for-One. Isn't it a lovely garage? The little red and yellow car sleeps there at night, as cosy as can be.

In the morning, Noddy wakes up, takes off his little pyjamas and has a bath in a tub he bought for himself, because he hasn't got a bathroom.

He looks funny in his bath, because his body is made of wood, and it's quite round. He looks very nice when he is dressed, though, especially when he puts on his cap with the tinkling bell.

He always sings when he brushes his mop of hair and cleans his shoes.

"I've cleaned my teeth
And I've brushed my hair,
I've polished my shoes
And I've time to spare
To drink my milk
And to eat my bread,
And I've plenty of time
To nod my head.
Nid-diddy-nod,
Nid-diddy-nod!"

It's a funny little song, and Mr and Mrs Tubby, the bears who live next door, like to hear it every morning.

One morning there was a knock at Noddy's little front door. "Hey, Noddy! Are you there? Get out your car and take me to the Village of Bouncing Balls, will you?"

Noddy opened the door. The clockwork clown was outside in the garden. He was going head-over-heels all over the place. That was the way he usually went along.

Noddy had often wound him up with his key to set him going – and over and over he went until he looked nothing but head and heels.

"Do stop, Clown," said Noddy. "You always make me feel so dizzy. Whatever do you want to go to the Village of Bouncing Balls for?"

"I want to get a little one for myself," said the clown, standing up for a moment. "I plan to do a good trick with it – walk on it all around the circus ring when I perform."

"I should hate to try to walk on a ball," said Noddy. "Oh, don't start going head-over-heels again. Look, you've squashed one of my plants."

The clown stood up again. "Are you ready?" he said. "Well, get your car out then. I'm in a hurry."

Noddy got his car out and the clown got in. "Now listen," said Noddy. "If you begin going head-over-heels in and out of the car, I'll leave you behind! You'd give me such a fright that I would run into a lamp post or something."

"All right," said the clown. "Though I would rather like to see you knock a lamp post down. BANG! What a noise it would make."

THE CLOCKWORK CLOWN KEPT GOING
HEAD OVER HEELS

"Now you're being silly," said Noddy, and away they went. The clown began to sing at the top of his voice.

> *"If I were a bouncing ball*
> *I'd bounce myself so high*
> *That I'd knock all the clouds away*
> *And make a hole in the sky."*

Noddy began to laugh. "Now don't you teach silly ideas to the bouncing balls," he said. "They're quite mad enough already."

"Here we are," said the clown, as he saw the balls bouncing in the distance. "We didn't take long to get here. Wait for me, Noddy, and I'll go and get a really nice little ball."

THE VILLAGE OF BOUNCING BALLS

THE clown got out of the car and went off, head-over-heels, as fast as ever he could. A ball bounced up and then bounced itself all round the car.

"Don't," said Noddy. "If you make a mistake and bounce on my car you'll squash it flat. And me, too."

Another ball came up and bounced round. Noddy didn't like it at all. He thought he would drive off and run his car down a little rabbit burrow. Then he would be safe.

But the balls bounced after him, and Noddy was so scared that he couldn't see where he was going. He ran straight into two little balls standing together in the road talking.

"Whooooooooooo!" said one of the balls, and Noddy gazed in dismay at a big dent he had made in the rubber ball. There was a hole there, too, and the "whooooo" noise was the air coming out.

"Oh, sorry," said Noddy – but in a trice all kinds of balls came bouncing up and surrounded the little car.

The clockwork clown came hurrying up, too, with a little ball bouncing beside him. "*Now* what have you done, Noddy?" he said. "Dented a ball? How careless of you! My word – how angry these balls look. Come on – we'd better go."

So off they went at top speed – but it was a horrid drive because all the balls did their best to bounce on top of the car. Noddy drove to and fro and zigzagged all the way, trying to get out of the way of the angry balls.

NODDY ZIGZAGGED ALL THE WAY, TRYING TO GET
OUT OF THE WAY OF THE ANGRY BALLS

One knocked the clown's hat off, and one made a car lamp crooked. Noddy drove as fast as he could, and at last they were out of Bouncing Ball Village. Only one ball was left, bouncing along merrily after the car.

"You needn't mind that one," said the clown. "It's the one I've got for myself – to perform that trick on, you know. It will follow us like a dog."

And so it did. Bouncity-bouncity-bounce, it went, and though Noddy was afraid it might bump into the car, it didn't.

The little nodding man was very, very glad when he got back to his own town again. "I shall never take anyone to the Village of Bouncing Balls again," he said. "It's too dangerous. You'll have to pay me double fare, Clown, for my trouble."

"Double, double,
For your trouble,
I'm quite willing,
Here's a shilling,"

said the clown, and handed over a nice round silver shilling. He got out and called to his little ball. It rolled up to him like a good, obedient little dog!

"No more bouncing, please," said the clown. "I want to practise walking on you. Now keep still and I'll jump up on you."

And away down the street the two of them went, the clown walking cleverly on the ball as it rolled along.

"I do hope it won't begin to bounce when the clown is walking on it," said Noddy to himself. "He *would* get a shock! Now I'll go and get some dinner. I really feel hungry after that peculiar visit to the Village of Bouncing Balls."

—◦◦ 4 ◦◦—

AT THE TOY FARM

ONE day Noddy got a message from Mr Straw, the farmer at the toy farm.

"Please will you come and fetch some of my hens and ducks and take them to market for me? My horse has hurt his leg and he can't take the farm cart to market."

"Well, it will be a change to take hens and ducks in my car instead of toys," said Noddy to himself. "I hope they'll be good."

He got to the farm. It was a dear little farm with a pond and a farmhouse and sheds and fences. Noddy was careful not to go too near the trees, because he knew they fell over very easily. He hooted outside the farmhouse door.

Mrs Straw, the farmer's wife, came to the door, smiling. "Oh, hallo, little Noddy," she said. "Can you drive your car over the fields to the hen-house there? Mr Straw has the hens and ducks ready."

Noddy drove carefully over the fields. He had to open a gate once and drive through it. And,

oh dear me, there was a goat there who didn't like Noddy coming into his field at all.

He ran at the car and butted it hard at the back. Up into the air it went, with Noddy in it, and right over the hedge!

Noddy fell out into the hedge, and the car fell splash into a pond. The ducks fled off the water, quacking in fear.

The farmer stared in surprise at Noddy. "Do you usually try to drive your car over hedges?" he said.

"It was your goat," said Noddy crossly. "Come and get me down, Mr Straw. I'm stuck up in this hedge. It's a very good thing that my body is wooden, or these prickles would be hurting me!"

Mr Straw got him down. They went and looked at the car. It was upside down in the water. Noddy felt very miserable indeed.

He and the farmer tried to get it out, but they couldn't. "You'll have to empty the pond," said Noddy. "I can't lose my car."

So Mr Straw called to all his cows and donkeys and sheep and pigs. "Buttercup, Daisy, Woolly, Long-Ears, come here, all of you!"

They all came, about twelve of them, and stood looking at the car in the pond.

ALL THE TOY FARM ANIMALS BENT THEIR HEADS
AND DRANK

"Drink," said Mr Straw. "Drink as much as you can. Quickly, now!"

So Buttercup, Daisy, Woolly, Long-Ears and all the rest of the toy farm animals bent their heads and drank.

The water sank lower and lower – and at last the pond was almost empty. "Your animals look very fat now," said Noddy, rather alarmed. "Tell them to stop. We can get the car now."

So the animals stopped drinking, and Mr Straw and Noddy tugged the little car the right way up, and then wheeled it to the bank, through the mud. Noddy was very dirty when he had finished, and so was Mr Straw.

"I must go home and have a bath," said Noddy. "And I must wash my car, too. Oh dear – what a dreadful morning. I'll be back for your hens and ducks this afternoon, Mr Straw."

Well, he went back that afternoon, quite clean, but as his clothes weren't dry, Mrs Tubby, the teddy bear next door, had lent him a pair of Mr Tubby's old blue trousers, which were much too big for him, and a little coat of her own. He really looked very peculiar.

"Just leave the hens with my brother at the market," said Mr Straw. "Here's sixpence for their fare. And if they lay any eggs on the way you can have them, to make up for my goat butting you."

The hens and ducks were all squashed together on the seat beside Noddy. They were excited about their ride, and quacked and clucked loudly.

"Now hold tightly," said Noddy. "And nobody is to fly off. Off we go!"

And off they went. One of the hens was frightened and crept onto Noddy's knee, which made it difficult for him to drive the car. He got to market, found Mr Straw's brother, and gave him all the excited birds.

Will you believe it — when Noddy got back into the car to drive home, there were eleven eggs on the seat beside him! Eleven! Noddy stared at them in delight.

"Eleven eggs for my breakfast!" he said. "No, ten, because I must give Mrs Tubby one for lending me these clothes. What a bit of luck!"

5

THE GOBLIN COMES

NODDY was really a very busy little taxi driver indeed. His car was used a dozen times a day for this and that.

He was so friendly and polite that everyone liked him. He gave the tiny dolls rides for nothing. He always picked up the little clockwork mouse when he saw him hurrying to catch the toy train. And if he met a pixie or a brownie he stopped to give them a lift.

And then one day a goblin called on him. "Are you Noddy, the little nodding man, who has a car?" asked the goblin, putting his head round the door and making Noddy jump.

"Yes. But please don't peep round like that. There's a knocker on the door," said Noddy. "What do you want?"

"I want to go to a party in the Dark Wood at midnight," said the goblin.

"Oh — I don't think I want to go to the Dark Wood in the middle of the night," said Noddy. "It's rather frightening there."

"I'll give you a bag of sixpences if you'll take me," said the goblin, and he jingled the money in his pocket. He looked round Noddy's little house. "They would buy you a new carpet, and a new armchair, and a much nicer clock."

A bag of sixpences! Dear, dear — that sounded

a lot of money. Noddy thought about it, nodding his head until the bell on his hat jingled a tune.

"All right," he said at last, "I'll take you. But I don't like it much. I've done hardly any driving at night, and my lamps aren't very good. And I really *don't* like the Dark Wood, even in the daytime."

34

"Pooh," said the goblin. "I'll be with you, won't I? You can come to the party, too, if you like, and take me back home. That will be two bags of sixpences then."

Noddy nodded his head madly. *Two* bags of sixpences! Why, he would be very, very rich – and all for a drive in the middle of the night to the Dark Wood. Who cared about the Dark Wood? Anyway, the moon would be shining.

At twelve o'clock that night Noddy got out his little car. He jumped when a voice came out of the darkness. "Are you ready? I'm here!"

It was the goblin. It was so dark that Noddy couldn't see him at all. Then Noddy took a step forwards and bumped straight into him.

"Oh, sorry," he said. "Yes, I'm ready. Here is the car. Jump in."

The goblin climbed in. Noddy switched on the lights of the little car. They weren't very good, only just enough to see by as he went down the streets of Toy Town. The goblin began to sing a peculiar song.

"It isn't very good
In the Dark Dark Wood
In the middle of the night
When there isn't any light;
It isn't very good
In the Dark Dark Wood."

IT WAS VERY DARK IN THE STREETS OF TOY TOWN

"Don't sing that," said Noddy. "You make me nervous. I shall drive into a tree or something. Be quiet, Goblin."

So the goblin was quiet, but he kept making little chuckling noises, which Noddy didn't like at all.

"I wish I hadn't come," he thought. "I do wish I hadn't come!"

—∾ 6 ∾—

IN THE DARK DARK WOOD

THEY came to the Dark Wood. Although the moon was shining in the sky, the wood was just like its name – very, very dark. The lights on Noddy's little car made little bright paths between the trees.

"Where's this party of yours?" asked Noddy. "I don't want to drive any deeper into the wood."

"Well, stop just here, then," said the goblin, and Noddy stopped. Where was the party? And the band? Where were the lights, and happy voices?

"It's so quiet," he said to the goblin. "Where *is* the party?"

"There isn't a party," said the goblin in a very nasty sort of voice. "This is a trap, Noddy.

We want your car for ourselves. Get out at once!"

Noddy couldn't move an inch. He was so full of alarm that he couldn't say a word. A trap! Whose trap? And why did they want his car?

Then things happened very quickly. Three ugly faces suddenly appeared in the light of the car's lamps, and three goblins came running to the car. In a trice they had hold of poor Noddy and pulled him right out of his little car.

The goblin who had come with him took the wheel, laughing loudly. "What did I tell you?" he said. "It isn't very good in the Dark Dark Wood! Hey, you others, there's room for one beside me and two sitting on the back of the car."

"Wait a minute," said one of the other goblins. "This little driver has got some rather nice clothes on. We might as well have those, too!"

"Oooh yes," said another goblin. "I'll have his lovely hat – it's got a jingle-bell at the top."

"And I'll have his shirt and tie," said a third goblin. He pulled them off poor little Noddy.

NODDY WRIGGLED AND SHOUTED AND WAILED

Then the driver leaned out and told the others to get him Noddy's dear little trousers and shoes.

Soon Noddy had no clothes on at all. He wriggled and shouted and wailed. "No, no, no! I want my hat, I want my shirt. You bad, wicked goblin! How dare you steal my things!"

But it wasn't a bit of good. What could the little nodding man do against four wicked goblins? Nothing at all.

The goblins piled into the little red and yellow car. Two were in front, two sat in the back of the car. One of them had Noddy's hat on. The moon shone down on it suddenly through the trees and Noddy wailed loudly.

"My dear little hat! Oh, do, do leave me that!"

"Ha, ha, ho, ho!" laughed the bad goblins and drove off at top speed. "R-r-r-r-r-r!" went the little car, and the sound grew fainter and fainter, till at last it couldn't be heard any more.

Noddy was all alone in the Dark Wood. He remembered the song of the goblin. "It isn't very good in the Dark Dark Wood," and he stood up, trembling.

"Help!" he called. "Oh, help, help, HELP! I'm little Noddy and I'm all alone and LOST!"

—⚬ 7 ⚬—

DEAR OLD BIG-EARS

NOBODY answered Noddy. He stumbled along through the trees, tears running down his cheeks.

> *"I've lost my hat,*
> *I've lost my car;*
> *I simply don't know*
> *Where they are!*
> *I'm all alone;*
> *Won't ANYBODY*
> *Come to help*
> *Poor little Noddy?"*

He went on and on until he met a scared little mouse hurrying back to his hole. "Mouse, mouse – tell me where I am!" called Noddy. "Does anyone live near here?"

"There's only M-m-m-mister B-b-b-big-Ears," said the mouse, frightened. "Over there, look — see that toadstool house in the moonlight?"

Noddy gave a sudden squeal of joy that scared the mouse so much he fled down a rabbit hole in mistake for his own hole. Noddy's head began to nod again. Oh, Big-Ears, Big-Ears, are you really near?

He came to the little toadstool house where Big-Ears lived, and his head nodded in joy. He banged at the front door in the stalk, yelling, "Big-Ears, Big-Ears, come and let me in!"

Big-Ears the brownie put his head out of the window and stared in surprise and alarm at the little nodding man outside.

"Noddy! Is it you? What are you doing here in the middle of the night without your clothes? Are you mad, or am I dreaming?"

"Let me *in*," shouted Noddy. "I'm cold without any clothes!"

So Big-Ears let him in and was soon hearing the sad story of how the goblins had laid a trap for poor Noddy and taken away his clothes and his car.

"Even my dear little hat with a bell," wept Noddy. "Oh, I'm so, so unhappy. Whooooo-shooo!"

"What a sneeze!" said Big-Ears, startled. "Look, I'll lend you a coat and we'll hurry back to Toy Town and get Mr Plod the policeman. Then you must go straight to bed, or you'll catch a dreadful chill."

So, wearing one of Big-Ears' coats, little Noddy hurried with his friend through the Dark Wood back to Toy Town. They woke up Mr Plod, and he was most astonished to hear their tale.

"A-whooooooosh-oooo!" sneezed Noddy again, and Big-Ears hurried him away, back to House-for-One, and put Noddy to bed with two hot water bottles.

"Now you can stay there, little Noddy," he said. "I'll soon put things right for you. What's the good of having a friend if he can't put things right?"

Noddy fell asleep. Big-Ears sat up in the chair and thought hard. How could he get everything back for Noddy? There must be some way. There always was a way to do something, if you wanted it badly enough.

In the morning, Noddy awoke to find Big-Ears bringing him his breakfast. "Now you stay in bed today, and look after that cold," said Big-Ears kindly. "Don't worry about anything. I've just had a very, very good idea, and if you are good and do what you're told I'll tell you presently."

The news soon got around Toy Town that Noddy had been robbed and was ill in bed. There were knocks on the door all day long!

"I'VE BROUGHT YOU SOME ROSES," SAID MRS TUBBY

"Can I come in?" called Mrs Tubby. "I've brought you some roses!"

"Can I come in?" cried someone else. "I've brought you an ice cream that must be eaten at once!" And in came Angela Golden-Hair, the pretty doll.

Rat-a-tat! In came the toy cat with a jigsaw puzzle to do. Rat-a-tat! That was the clockwork clown with two bananas and a peach. Rat-a-tat-TAT! That was Mr Straw with six brown eggs. Dear me, what a lot of friends Noddy has, to be sure!

"Oh, thank you, thank you, thank you," Noddy kept saying, and his head nodded happily. "I *am* having a lovely time!"

---⚬ 8 ⚬---

BIG-EARS HAS A VERY GOOD IDEA

WHEN everyone had gone, Noddy called to Big-Ears. "Tell me your very, very good idea, Big-Ears, please."

Big-Ears proudly showed him a big notice. This was what he had printed on it:

WILL ANYONE WHO HEARS A BELL JINGLING PLEASE TELL BIG-EARS?

"Ooh – you mean the bell on my hat?" said Noddy. "You think a goblin is wearing it – and it will jingle and give away their hiding place? Oooh, what a very, very good idea!"

Well it really was, because not half an hour after Big-Ears had put up the notice outside the little nodding man's house, two small clockwork mice came shyly in.

"Please, Mr Big-Ears," said one, "we've heard a bell jingling."

"Yes – we heard it inside the old hollow tree at the edge of the Dark Wood," whispered the other little mouse. "Not far from the stream, Mr Big-Ears."

"Thank you," said Big-Ears, delighted. "That is just what I wanted to know. Here's a bit of cheese for both of you."

The clockwork mice ran off, pleased. Big-Ears smiled at Noddy. "*Now* we know where those wicked goblins are hiding – in that old hollow tree. And now I come to think of it, there's a hole at the bottom of the tree where they could hide the car. Ha! I'll go and tell Mr Plod the policeman at once!"

Off he went, and Noddy was so excited that his head nodded twice as fast as he lay in bed waiting for the next bit of news.

Mr Plod said he would only want a big toy dog, a very large sack, himself and Big-Ears. So they set off with Bongo, the largest toy dog in Toy Town, and a big sack over the policeman's shoulder.

"Ssh!" said Big-Ears, when they came near the hollow tree. "Just send Bongo to bark at the bottom hole. Climb up to the other hole, and I'll come with you. Bongo will bark and frighten the goblins, and they will all climb quickly out of the top hole into our sack!"

Bongo ran to the hole at the bottom of the tree and barked loudly. You should have heard him!

"Wuff, wuff, wuffy WUFF! WOOF, WOOF, WOOF! I'm hungry and I want a goblin. WOOF, WOOF!"

There was a loud noise from inside the tree, as the goblins began to climb up in a fright. There were squeals and howls and wails. There was a scrabbling noise as the four goblins scrambled up to the top hole.

Big-Ears was there, holding up the sack with Mr Plod. Plop! Plop! That was two goblins in the sack.

Plop! That was another. PLOP! That was the last one, and the biggest of them all.

"Tie them up," said Mr Plod, and he and Big-Ears tied up the neck of the sack very tightly indeed.

"Now I'll get Noddy's little car," said Big-Ears, and he scrambled down, went into the hole at the bottom – and, sure enough, there was Noddy's tiny car! Big-Ears wheeled it out.

"If you'd like to put the sack of goblins in the car you can drive them off to the police station," said Big-Ears. "I'll go and get my bicycle and follow you. There wouldn't be room for me. My house is just nearby."

So the policeman drove off with the sack of squealing, squirming goblins, and Big-Ears followed on his little bicycle, ringing the bell loudly.

"PLOP, PLOP!" WENT THE GOBLINS INTO THE SACK

They stopped outside House-for-One. Mr Plod hooted the horn. Parp-parp! Big-Ears rang his bell – ring-ring-ring-ring!

Noddy jumped out of bed and came to the window. "Hello, there!" shouted Big-Ears. "We've got a sack of goblins, and your car – and you'll soon have all your clothes back, too, once we've popped the goblins into prison!"

Noddy's head almost nodded itself off in joy. "Hurry back with my clothes," he cried, "especially my little hat — and bring back a big, big cake, Big-Ears. We'll have a party because you've been so very, very clever!"

And so they did. Big-Ears came back and gave Noddy all his clothes again. He drove the little car safely back into its garage, and then they both had a big slice of cake.

Big-Ears waved the cake knife in the air and began a happy song.

> *"It's a very happy thing*
> *When you've simply got to sing,*
> *Hey-derry-ho-derry,*
> *Loud as anything!"*

And Noddy joined in too, his bell ringing and his head nodding.

You can sing the song, too, if you want. Noddy and Big-Ears will be delighted!

Goodbye, little Noddy; goodbye, Big-Ears. See you again soon!